THE MOST FUN YOU'LL EVER HAVE!
REDS HEADS
REDS
REDS.COM/KIDSCLUB
REDS HEADS: AGES 3–12
REDS.COM/ROOKIES
REDS ROOKIES: 0–36 MONTHS
Reds
FOR MORE INFORMATION, VISIT reds.com

Like a lot of kids growing up, I played many different sports depending on the season, but there was always something special about baseball. Even though I grew up in Georgia surrounded by Braves fans, my favorite player was Barry Larkin. He made so many great plays as shortstop, and I always tried to mimic him when I was in the field. I always hoped I could grow up to be a big leaguer just like him.

As I look back on those memories today, I'm so thrilled that I get to wear a Reds uniform just like my idol did and even play here at Great American Ball Park where Barry played his final two seasons. I'm sure there are a lot of young Reds fans out there hoping they can grow up to be a baseball player just like I did when I was a kid. That's why I know all of you will enjoy reading this book because it gives you an inside look at Great American Ball Park. As you follow Gapper around, it's a chance to see behind the scenes of a Major League ballpark, something I know I would've loved as a kid.

Keep those big-league dreams alive out there and I look forward to seeing you all back at the ballpark again soon!

-Brandon Phillips

For the people and families of Reds Country and all Reds fans past, present, and future. For little Megan and my wife, Ashley.

Special Thanks:
It is an honor for me to have the opportunity to work with the Reds and to bring Reds fans a fun and informative book about Great American Ball Park. I would like to thank Karen Forgus, Lori Watt, Ralph Mitchell, Jarrod Rollins, and Michael Anderson of the Reds front office. Special thanks to Rick Stowe and Nick St. Pierre for all of their help and to Brandon Phillips for taking the time to write the foreword for this book. I also want to recognize all of the staff and employees of Great American Ball Park who work to bring Reds fans a fun, safe, and exciting place to come watch our team. This is our home...this is Reds Country!

- Joel Altman

Gapper's Grand Tour

A Voyage through Great American Ball Park

By Joel Altman

Illustrated by Tim Williams

MR. REDLEGS

IT'S SOMEONE'S FIRST GAME!

On another beautiful day in Cincinnati, Gapper arrived at Great American Ball Park early in the morning to meet his mascot friends and to get ready for the game that evening. As Gapper suited up inside the mascots' locker room, he didn't see Mr. Redlegs, Rosie Red, or Mr. Red. He decided to walk around the ballpark until he found them.

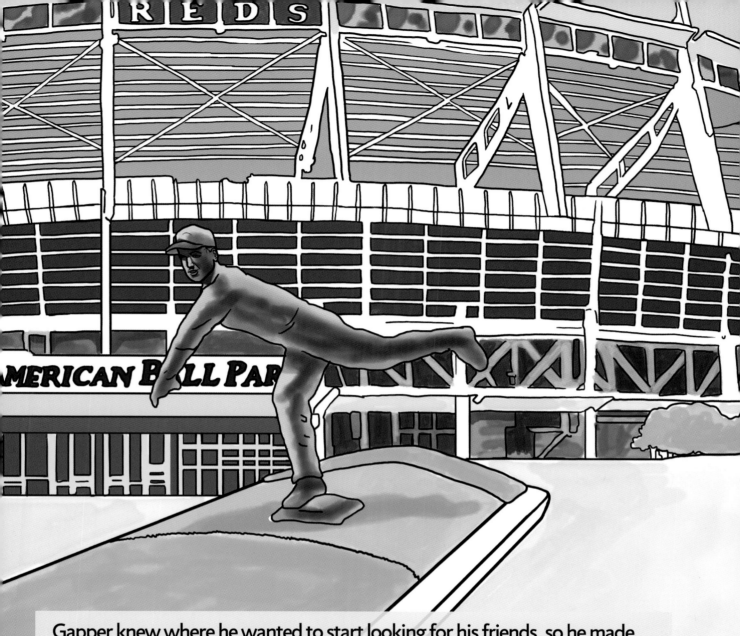

Gapper knew where he wanted to start looking for his friends, so he made his way up to the main entrance of Great American Ball Park which is called Crosley Terrace. This is where the Reds pay tribute to some of the most memorable players from the team's days at Crosley Field. Gapper looked around in awe at the four bronze statues that are frozen in time on the mock infield and pitcher's mound. Gapper was able to get up close and get a good view of Ted Kluszewski in the on deck circle, catcher Ernie Lombardi, pitcher Joe Nuxhall, and batter Frank Robinson. Gapper wondered what it would have been like to play with these amazing players!

Next, Gapper thought that his friends would definitely be in the Fan Zone. That is where they can usually be found during the games, hanging out and meeting their fans. Gapper can remember when the area that is now the Fan Zone was built on the site of the Reds previous home, Riverfront Stadium. The Fan Zone has a playground, the Reds Heads Kids Clubhouse, and the miniature turf field where fans can run the bases.

Also nearby, Gapper looked in the Rose Garden where the exact spot of Pete Rose's hit #4192 landed and is marked with a white rose bush. Gapper remembers learning about the day at Riverfront Stadium when Pete Rose broke Ty Cobb's all-time hit record to become baseball's Hit King! While Gapper was exploring the Fan Zone, he started to get hungry, so he stopped by Mr. Red's Smokehouse to get some barbecue. He made a huge mess!

Gapper had no luck finding his friends in the Fan Zone, so he decided to head up to the Riverfront Club where he could get a good view of inside the ballpark and the surrounding area. If his friends are around, Gapper should definitely be able to see them from up here! Inside the Riverfront Club, Gapper saw a sight that is unlike any in the ballpark. Not only could he see the field and enjoy the gourmet food, but Gapper also saw a view of the Ohio River and Northern Kentucky that was amazing!

Gapper could see Newport on the Levee. He watched the old-style riverboats go by and had a beautiful view of the Roebling Suspension Bridge which opened to pedestrians in 1866. That is even older than the Reds baseball team! Gapper was also able to look over the area between Great American Ball Park and the Bengals' Paul Brown Stadium.

This area, known as the Banks, is home to many new restaurants and shops in downtown Cincinnati. As he looked around, Gapper couldn't wait to visit all of these wonderful places!

After leaving the Riverfront Club, Gapper decided to go to the Press Box to see if anyone there was conducting a TV interview of his mascot friends. Once Gapper arrived, he didn't see them, but he sat down to pretend that he was a big-shot TV broadcaster reporting on the game that night.

Gapper thought he could comment on how he likes to make sure that every fan has a good time. When he meets a fan who's at their first Reds game, he wants to help them become a Reds fan for life.

From the Press Box, Gapper could see the booth where Marty Brennaman broadcasts Reds games on the radio. Gapper thought that he could go over and use the radio to put a broadcast out for his mascot friends in case they were listening. As Gapper made his way inside the radio booth, he saw plaques honoring Marty, Joe Nuxhall, and Waite Hoyt, who have broadcasted Reds games for generations of fans.

As Gapper looked around and was playing with the microphone, Marty came into the room and yelled, "Gapper! Stop goofing around before you break something!" Gapper quickly ran down the hall before doing any real damage.

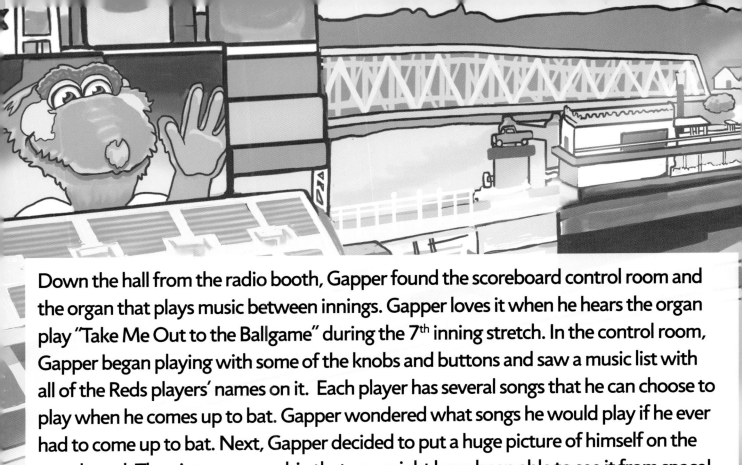

Down the hall from the radio booth, Gapper found the scoreboard control room and the organ that plays music between innings. Gapper loves it when he hears the organ play "Take Me Out to the Ballgame" during the 7th inning stretch. In the control room, Gapper began playing with some of the knobs and buttons and saw a music list with all of the Reds players' names on it. Each player has several songs that he can choose to play when he comes up to bat. Gapper wondered what songs he would play if he ever had to come up to bat. Next, Gapper decided to put a huge picture of himself on the scoreboard. The picture was so big that you might have been able to see it from space! Gapper then decided to play some music on the organ but it sounded awful because Gapper doesn't know how to play any music. Gapper decided he better leave the area before anyone saw him messing around.

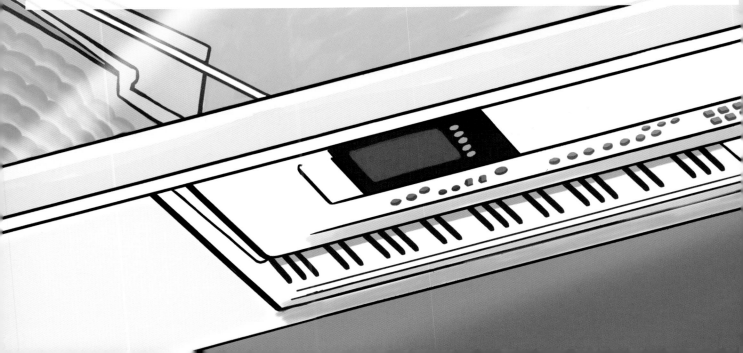

To continue the search for his friends, Gapper decided to head back downstairs to the tunnels underneath the ballpark that lead to the Reds Clubhouse. The tunnel is so big that you could drive a truck through it and goes all the way around in one big loop. Gapper looked around and saw the banners on each side of the entrance to the Clubhouse that represent each World Series Championship that the Reds have won. Gapper is hoping that this year they can add another banner to the wall!

Gapper decided to check out the Clubhouse to see if his friends might be inside, so he quietly opened the door and snuck inside. Gapper was awestruck at how bright and welcoming it was. Each player has their own chair and there are couches and TVs all around so the players can relax before the game.

Gapper was getting tired so he decided to relax on a couch when the Reds manager, Dusty Baker, came in and said, "Gapper! What are you doing in here? Shouldn't you be getting ready for the game?" Gapper quickly ran away from the area and headed down the hallway that leads to the Reds dugout...

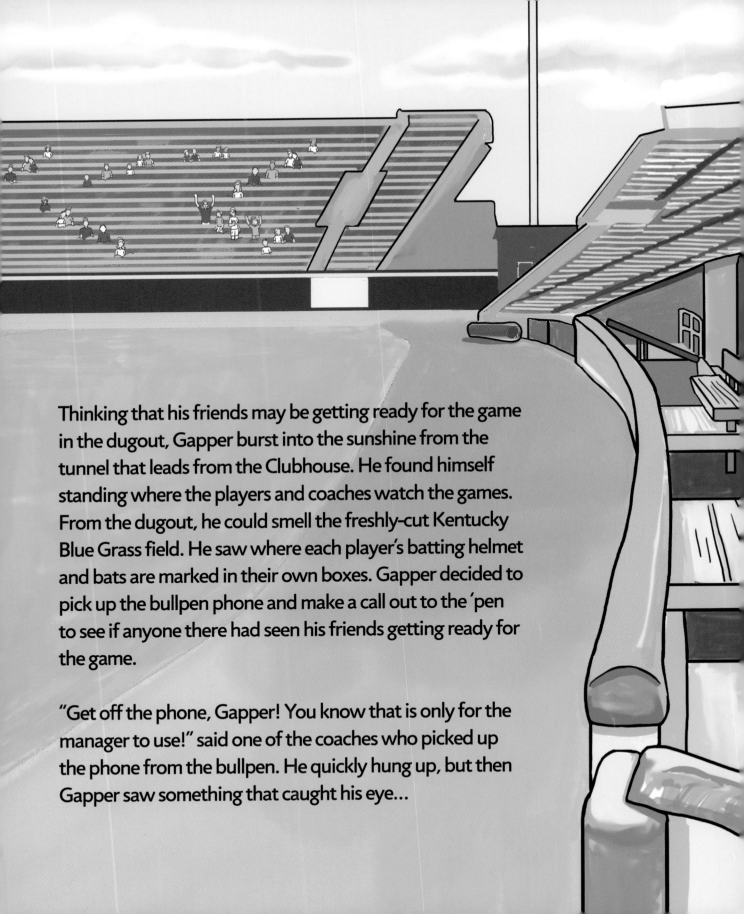

Thinking that his friends may be getting ready for the game in the dugout, Gapper burst into the sunshine from the tunnel that leads from the Clubhouse. He found himself standing where the players and coaches watch the games. From the dugout, he could smell the freshly-cut Kentucky Blue Grass field. He saw where each player's batting helmet and bats are marked in their own boxes. Gapper decided to pick up the bullpen phone and make a call out to the 'pen to see if anyone there had seen his friends getting ready for the game.

"Get off the phone, Gapper! You know that is only for the manager to use!" said one of the coaches who picked up the phone from the bullpen. He quickly hung up, but then Gapper saw something that caught his eye...

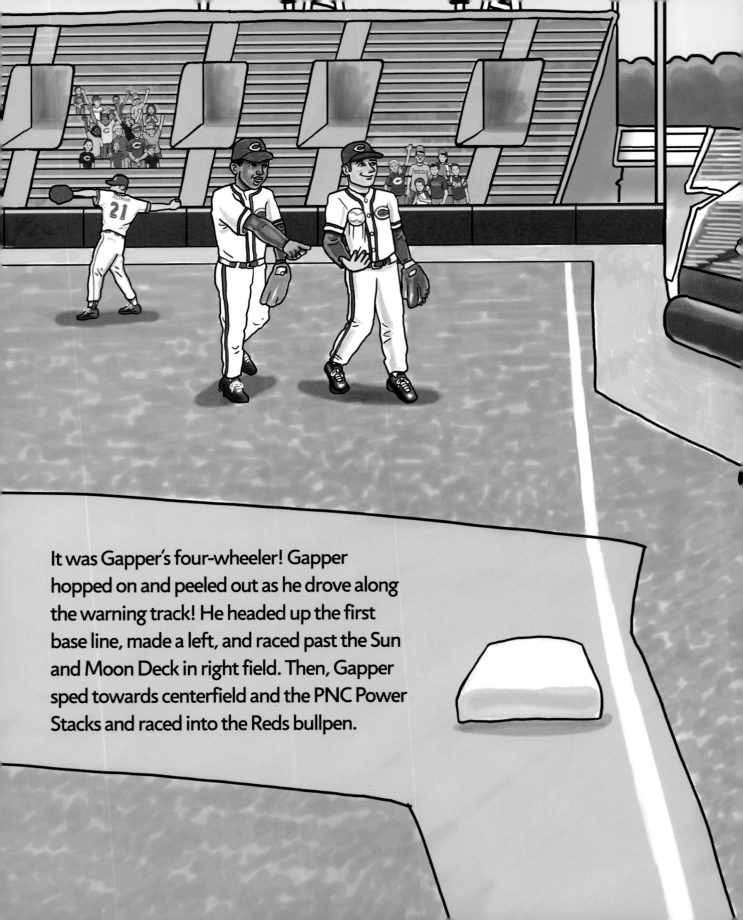

It was Gapper's four-wheeler! Gapper hopped on and peeled out as he drove along the warning track! He headed up the first base line, made a left, and raced past the Sun and Moon Deck in right field. Then, Gapper sped towards centerfield and the PNC Power Stacks and raced into the Reds bullpen.

Wow! That was fun! thought Gapper as he picked up a bucket of baseballs and began to warm up his arm like a Reds pitcher. Gapper wished that he could throw that fast!

"Gapper, we need to get ready for the game, what are you doing?" asked the Reds catcher.

After Gapper threw a few pitches in the bullpen, he hopped back on his four-wheeler and headed back out along the warning track. He launched past the scoreboard in left field and then shot down the third base line like a rocket.

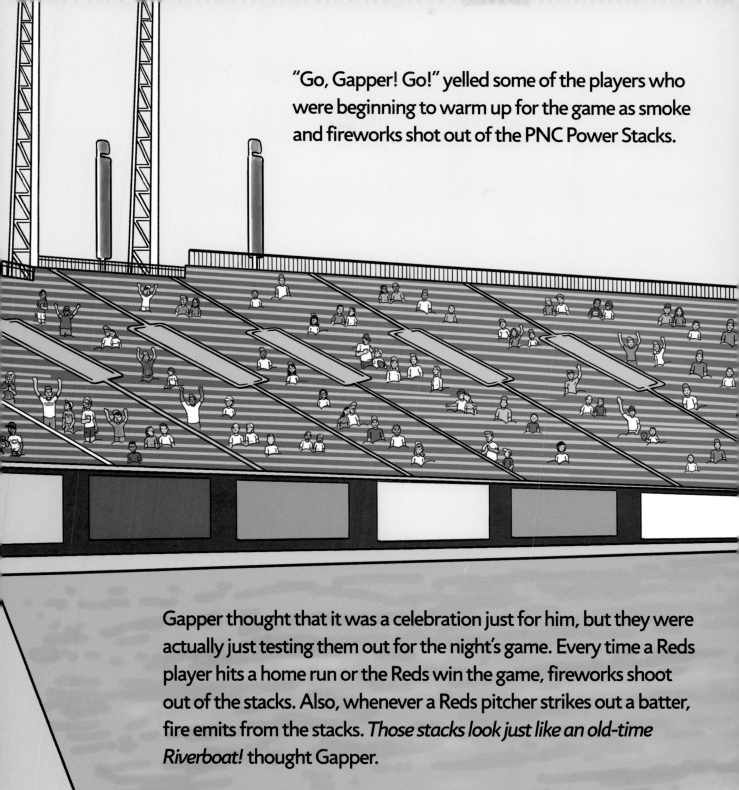

"Go, Gapper! Go!" yelled some of the players who were beginning to warm up for the game as smoke and fireworks shot out of the PNC Power Stacks.

Gapper thought that it was a celebration just for him, but they were actually just testing them out for the night's game. Every time a Reds player hits a home run or the Reds win the game, fireworks shoot out of the stacks. Also, whenever a Reds pitcher strikes out a batter, fire emits from the stacks. *Those stacks look just like an old-time Riverboat!* thought Gapper.

Gapper screeched to a halt in front of the visiting team's dugout. It was almost game time and Gapper was really worried that he had not found any of his mascot friends yet.

He hopped off of his four-wheeler and made his way down the visiting dugout stairs. Thinking maybe he would find his friends in the umpires' dressing room, Gapper peeked inside.

One of the umpires spotted him and yelled, "Gapper! No one is allowed in the umpires' dressing room except for umpires! You're outta here!"

Gapper quickly shut the door and ran back out onto the field.

As Gapper came back onto the field, he was worried that he wouldn't find his friends anywhere and the game was about to begin. Then, he jumped for joy when he saw Mr. Red, Rosie Red, and Mr. Redlegs waiting by the pitcher's mound.

"Gapper, where have you been?" asked Mr. Redlegs.

Gapper tried to explain that he was looking for them all day and couldn't find them.

"Well, we were in the one place you didn't look," said Rosie Red.

"We were in the Reds Hall of Fame and Museum all day, Gapper!" added Mr. Red. "You are such a goof, Gapper! We always go to the Museum on game days!"

Gapper was excited just to be with his friends again. They hoisted him up into the air as he threw out the first pitch! What a day at Great American Ball Park!

Reds™ FUN FACTS:

- The organ Gapper plays on originally came from Riverfront Stadium and was moved over to GABP when the stadium opened in 2003.
- The field is a mix of Kentucky Blue Grass and Rye Seed that is grown in Southeast Indiana.
- During the season, the head groundskeeper often sleeps at the ballpark to make sure the field is always in perfect condition. Now that's dedication!
- The statues in Crosley Terrace were sculpted by local artist Thomas Tsuchiya. New statues are planned for future release.
- Home plate was dug up from Riverfront Stadium and transported after the final game there on September 22, 2002. Home plate now stands 580 feet from the Ohio River.
- Great American Ball Park has field dimensions of 328 feet in left field, 404 in center field, and 325 feet in right field.
- All of the seats in the ballpark are actually angled towards home plate to give each fan a comfortable view of the action.
- The main scoreboard was installed in 2009 and is a full true High Definition board which is 137-by-38 feet.
- There are several different sections of seats where you can watch the game from, including the Kroger Bleachers in left field, the Cincinnati Bell Riverboat Deck in center field, and the Sun and Moon Deck in right field, which was influenced by the stands at Crosley Field.
- Great American Ball Park has 31 concession stands, as well as the Riverfront Club, Diamond Club, FOX Sports Ohio Champions Club, and the Machine Room Grille.
- The Reds Hall of Fame and Museum opened in 2004 and is right next to the ballpark. It's open year-round and has a wide variety of permanent exhibits, along with new featured exhibits each season. Gapper and his friends know that he should go there every game day to look at all the exciting displays!